Disney's
The
ARISTOCATS
Get Into Mischief

GROLIER
BOOK CLUB EDITION

First American Edition
Copyright © 1979 by The Walt Disney Company.
All rights reserved under International and
Pan-American Copyright Conventions.
Published in the United States by
Random House, Inc., New York,
and simultaneously in Canada by
Random House of Canada Limited, Toronto.
Originally published in Denmark as
ARISTOCATS: KILLINGERNE PA GALE VEJE
by Gutenberghus Bladene, Copenhagen.
Copyright © 1979 by Walt Disney Productions
ISBN: 0-394-84229-4 (trade), ISBN: 0-394-94229-9 (lib. bdg.)
Manufactured in the United States of America

Duchess was a very pretty cat.

She was the mother of three sweet kittens named Tu-Tu, Berly, and Marie.

They all lived in a fine old house with Madame, a very rich old lady.

Every morning Madame tied clean bows
on the kittens.

Every evening she gave them bowls of cream.

Madame loved her four
beautiful cats.
And they loved her.

Duchess was a perfect cat.
She taught her kittens to be
perfect, too.

Marie learned to hold her head high when she walked.

Tu-Tu learned to sit up straight.

Berly learned to run fast without knocking anything over.

But when Tom O'Malley came to live with them, everything changed.

O'Malley was a big, strong alley cat.

The kittens thought O'Malley was wonderful.

They wanted to be just like him when they grew up.

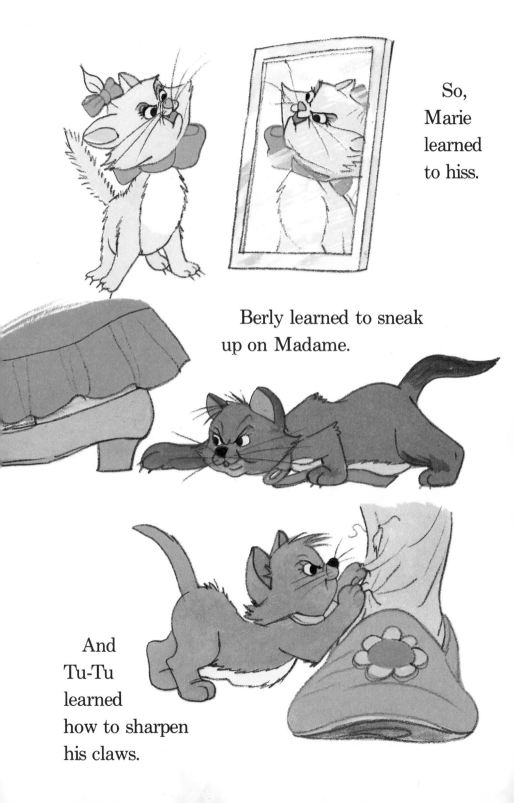

So, Marie learned to hiss.

Berly learned to sneak up on Madame.

And Tu-Tu learned how to sharpen his claws.

The kittens grew wilder and wilder.

One day they even knocked over Madame's favorite plant.

"Oh Duchess," cried Madame, "what is happening to these kittens?"

Duchess was mad at O'Malley.

"It is all your fault," she said. "You are teaching them your alley-cat ways."

O'Malley did not like what Duchess said, but he promised to be good.

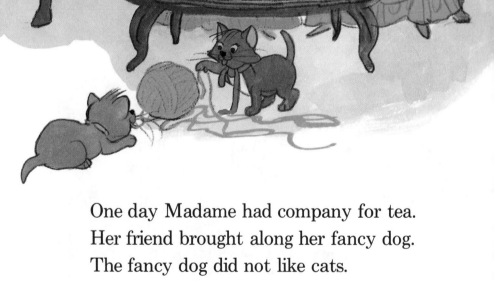

One day Madame had company for tea.
Her friend brought along her fancy dog.
The fancy dog did not like cats.
He did not bother Duchess or the kittens,
but he growled at O'Malley.

O'Malley
growled
right
back.

Then the dog tried to bite O'Malley.
That was too much!
O'Malley jumped on the dog.
There was a terrible fight, and
Madame's tea tray crashed
to the floor.

"Oh, what a horrid cat," cried Madame's friend.

Then she walked out of the house.

Madame was very angry.

"Tom O'Malley," she said, "this house is not a back alley!"

O'Malley did not think it was his fault.
The fancy dog started the trouble.
But Madame and Duchess were both angry at him.
"I might as well move out," he said sadly.
The three kittens watched him leave.

"I do not want O'Malley to go away," said Marie.
"But what can we do?" said Berly.
"Let's follow him," said Tu-Tu. "We'll be
alley cats, too!"

And off they ran.

O'Malley walked to town.
He did not notice the kittens following him.

It was pleasant walking
through the park at night.
O'Malley began to feel better.

Suddenly he turned and saw the kittens.
"You should not be here," he said
sternly. "Now go home."

Then he went
on his way again.

But the kittens did not want to go home.

They wanted to be with O'Malley, so they kept on following him.

Suddenly O'Malley heard music.

He stopped and looked around the corner.

It was a group of his old friends.

"It's O'Malley! Hey, man," said the cool cat in the blue hat.

That was O'Malley's friend Scat Cat.

Then O'Malley saw the kittens hiding behind
a trash can.

"I thought I told you to go home," he said.

"Those are okay kittens," said Cyril, the
guitar player. "Let them stay, O'Malley."

So the kittens were allowed to stay.

O'Malley joined the band and played the washboard.

Marie, Berly, and Tu-Tu had a great time.
They danced and sang,
"Dooby, dooby, dooby dee,
An alley cat is happy and free."

The cats made a lot of noise.

The neighbors were furious.

They threw flowerpots, bottles, carrots, and shoes at the cats.

One old shoe knocked off Scat Cat's hat.

"Stop that noise!"
the people shouted.
One man even
dumped water out
the window.

"Let's get out of
here," O'Malley said,
and off they ran.

It started to rain.

O'Malley and the kittens sat inside
a big pipe to stay dry.

The kittens were cold and hungry, but they
were still happy to be with O'Malley.

When it stopped
raining, O'Malley
said, "Come on. I will
show you the city
from up high."

The kittens had
never climbed a fire
escape before.

"See? There it is," said O'Malley.

"Gee," said Tu-Tu, "you can see everything from up here."

Then it started to rain again.
Water rushed out of the drainpipe.
Suddenly the kittens were slipping.
"Help," they cried.

O'Malley grabbed for the kittens.
One, two, three!
He scooped them up
just in time.

"That was close," O'Malley said.
"This life is too dangerous for you
kittens. I will take you home."

He led the kittens down
the fire escape and back
onto the street.

It was getting late.
Marie was very tired, so O'Malley
carried her.

The kittens were so happy
to see Madame's house.

O'Malley took them up
to the front door.

Then he walked away quietly.

He thought Madame and
Duchess were still mad at him.

When Madame heard the kittens mewing,
she opened the door.

"Oh, my dear little kittens," she said.
"You have come back! But where is Tom
O'Malley?"

Madame picked up
all three kittens
and hugged them.

She washed them
and dried them with
clean towels.

She gave them each a bowl of cream.

But Duchess had seen O'Malley.
She ran after him.

"Oh, I want
you to stay,"
she said.

"And the kittens need a father
to look after them."

Madame and
Duchess were
happy because
the family was
together again.

The kittens were happy, too.

They had had enough adventures to last
them for a while.

Even O'Malley was happy, because Madame
and Duchess had forgiven him.

And he had forgiven them.

"Home, sweet home," he sighed.